The Sunbeam and the Wave

Also by Connie Bowen

I Believe in Me

Yo creo en mí

I Turn to the Light

The Sunbeam

and the

Wave

Harriet Elizabeth Hamilton

Illustrations by Connie Bowen

Unity House

Unity Village, Missouri

This original story of a sunbeam and a wave was inspired by a passage from *A Course in Miracles* titled "The Little Garden."

First Edition 2000

A **WeeWisdom** Book
for the child within us all

To receive a catalog of all Unity publications (books, cassettes, compact discs, and magazines) or to place an order, call the Customer Service Department (816) 969-2069 or 1-800-669-0282.

The publisher wishes to acknowledge the editorial work of Raymond Teague and Michael Maday; the copy services of Kay Thomure, Beth Anderson, and Deborah Dribben; the production help of Rozanne Devine and Jane Blackwood; and the marketing efforts of Allen Liles, Jenee Meyer, and Sharon Sartin.

Cover design by Gretchen West

Library of Congress Cataloging-in-Publication Data
Hamilton, Harriet Elizabeth, 1942-
    The sunbeam and the wave / Harriet Elizabeth Hamilton ;
illustrations by Connie Bowen. -- 1st ed.
    p.   cm.
    SUMMARY: Two friends, Sunbeam and Wave, learn that they are each part of something greater than themselves.
    ISBN 0-87159-250-9 (alk. paper)
    [1. Ocean Fiction. 2. Sunshine Fiction. 3. Friendship Fiction.]
I. Bowen, Connie, ill. II. Title.
    PZ7.H1818 Su 2000
    [E] -- dc21
Canada BN 13252 9033 RT

99 - 16282
CIP

Dedication

To my teachers, Sri Svami Purna, Jesus, and the Great Central Sun.
May I reflect Your Light, Lord
As the Moon reflects the Light of the Sun
In love, always in Love.
—HH

To Ellen
—CB

Once upon a time there was a beautiful, sparkling Sunbeam who lived on the crest of a bouncy little Wave in the Ocean.

The tiny Sunbeam and the little Wave were best friends, so they spent every day together, talking and playing.

"Look at me," the little Wave would sometimes boast. "See how big I am? I am as big as the entire Ocean." And then he would stretch himself up into a huge wave, and the tiny Sunbeam would be very impressed. She would sigh with admiration, which always made him very proud.

The tiny Sunbeam felt honored to know a wave as mighty as the entire Ocean. But she did not want to appear any less important, so she would polish her sparkles, point her little nose up in the air, and reply confidently: "Of course you are. And I am the most beautiful light in the whole world, and the brightest too." And the little Wave, who really did think she was beautiful, would always agree whole-heartedly.

On sunny afternoons the tiny Sunbeam liked nothing better than to take a short walk along the crest of the little Wave. She was very careful and always looked where she was going.

"Now be still and don't move around too much," she would say. "I don't want to fall off, for who knows what would become of me? You wouldn't want anything to happen to the most beautiful light in all the world, now would you?"

"No, of course not," the little Wave would reply. And he would take great care to be smooth and gentle and not move around too much, even though it tickled.

There were other sunbeams who lived on nearby waves, but the tiny Sunbeam always pretended she didn't see them. "What if they are brighter than I am? Then maybe my little Wave would like them better. It would be terrible to lose my best friend," she thought to herself.

Although she kept it a secret, there was one other thing she was afraid of—the Great Light in the Daytime Sky. She never looked at it, for that light was so bright that she had decided it must surely devour tiny sunbeams. So she never spoke of it, not even to herself.

But in spite of these fears, the two friends spent the days happily bobbing up and down across the Ocean.

At sunset, when the Great Light in the Daytime Sky disappeared over the horizon, the tiny Sunbeam would yawn and slowly fade away. She never wondered where it was she went or how it was she reappeared the next day. She just knew that's the way it was, because that's the way it had always been.

But the little Wave wondered. Sometimes he felt so alone that he couldn't sleep at all and spent the entire night adrift on the dark, endless Ocean, with no one to talk to. Sometimes he pouted. "Why does she always leave me? If she really cared about me, she wouldn't go. Maybe she doesn't really like me very much after all." But he kept his feelings to himself and never told anyone.

One evening, just as he was about to fall asleep, the little Wave became aware of something that was tickling him! Yes, it was definitely a tickle, out in the middle of the Ocean, and at bedtime too!

Oh, he did his best to ignore it, but as soon as he would get comfortable, that tickle would come back again. His curiosity got the best of him, and the little Wave opened first one eye and then the other and then raised straight up in his ocean bed. Just then the loveliest, palest light he had ever seen bounced across the water with a laugh, stepped on his nose, and did a somersault right down his back, without even stopping to say "Excuse me."

"Wh-what was that?" he sputtered. He watched as she bounced from wave to wave, laughing as if she didn't have a care in the world. "Whoever she is, she sure is having fun," he thought. So when she came back, he spoke to her.

"Excuse me, uh, excuse me, would you stop for a minute? I want to ask you a question," he ventured in his most polite voice.

"Sure!" giggled the Moonbeam.

"Who are you?" asked the little Wave. "Where do you come from?"

"Why," laughed the Moonbeam, "I am a reflection of the Great Light in the Nighttime Sky. Haven't you ever seen her shining? She is very beautiful, and my sisters and I are beautiful too, because we are her reflections."

And with that she went skipping along the top of the little Wave, bouncing merrily to one side and then the other. Nothing seemed to bother her—not getting splashed in the face or getting her feet wet or even falling headfirst into the water.

"You … you mean there's more than just one of you?" asked the little Wave, turning to follow her.

"Just one, but we look like many," giggled the Moonbeam, without bothering to turn around. "Look around you and you'll see." And he heard giggles all around him, as tiny specks of light jumped gingerly from one wave to another on the sleepy Ocean.

"Just one, but you look like many? How is that?" asked the little Wave.

The Moonbeam didn't answer. She merely turned her face upward to the Great Light in the Nighttime Sky and smiled. Then she bounced off without a care in the world.

"Be careful—you might fall off!" cautioned the little Wave, remembering his Sunbeam. "And then what would become of you?"

Peals of laughter came from the Moonbeam and her sisters. "Silly little Wave, what could ever happen to us? We are reflections!" And with that she began playing hopscotch, jumping from one imaginary point to another, and squealing with delight.

The little Wave thought for most of the night about what she had said. He wondered, if the Moonbeam was a reflection of the Great Light in the Nighttime Sky, did that mean that his Sunbeam was a part of the Great Light in the Daytime Sky? He decided to ask her in the morning, and with that, he, too, fell asleep.

The next day, as soon as the Sunbeam had finished all of her usual primping, the little Wave asked if he could speak to her about something important.

"Of course," glowed the tiny Sunbeam, and she sat down, taking care not to get too close to the edge, for then she might fall off and disappear forever.

Gathering all the determination he had, the little Wave told her about what had happened the night before. In his exuberance, he blurted out all of his questions at once.

"Where do you go every night, and what do you do while you're there? Are you a part of the Great Light in the Daytime Sky, like the reflections of the Great Light in the Nighttime Sky, who come and play on the Ocean at night? Tell me about this Great Light in the Daytime Sky and about all the other sunbeams too. Are they your sisters?"

The tiny Sunbeam's face clouded over with anger. "Whatever is the matter with you, asking such silly questions!" she scolded. "I've never heard such nonsense in all of my life," and she turned her back, folded her arms, and stomped angrily up and down the crest of the little Wave.

"Where do I go at night? I don't go anywhere at night, except to sleep! Where do you go, that you hear such silly stories about *reflections*?" she sparked, pointing her little nose up and closing her eyes.

"Reflections, indeed!" she bristled. "I've never even heard of these, these *reflections* you talk about. You probably made them up just to make me jealous.

"I don't know anything about a Great Light in the Daytime Sky. Why would you make up such an awful story when *I* am the brightest and most beautiful light in all the world?" she asked accusingly.

And with that the tiny Sunbeam sat down and started to cry. She sniffed and sobbed and pouted for the whole day and wouldn't say a single word to the little Wave.

However, the next morning the Sunbeam began chattering again as usual. The little Wave felt confused. But both pretended there was nothing bothering them.

One morning, as the tiny Sunbeam primped and admired herself on the crest of the Wave, something felt funny. She looked up and saw that the sky was not its usual blue color. There were some dark shapes in the distance.

"Little Wave, my friend, look over there," she said with a frightened voice and pointed. "What are those?"

"Those are clouds," replied the little Wave. "They live in the sky."

14

"But they look dark and mean," she said. "I am afraid of them. Make them go away."

"Make them go away? But how?" the little Wave asked. "I don't know how to make clouds go away."

"But you are as mighty as the Ocean," she countered. "You can do anything. You are the mightiest being on the Earth. You told me so yourself. Make them go away!" she demanded.

The little Wave didn't know how to make the dark clouds go away, but he *had* told the Sunbeam that he was as mighty as the Ocean. He was afraid to tell her that it wasn't the truth, because then he would look foolish.

"What can I do now?" he thought. "She won't want to be my friend anymore if she finds out that I'm only an ordinary wave."

So, while the Sunbeam hid behind one of his ripples, he asked the Wind for some advice.

"Excuse me, sir," said the little Wave politely. "Can you help me?"

"What do you want?" gusted the Wind. "I am very busy right now."

"I-I wa-want to know how to scare those dark clouds away," stammered the little Wave timidly. "My Sunbeam is very frightened of them, and she wants them to go away."

"You can't make them go away," blew the Wind. "They are storm clouds, and I am blowing them this way to bring rain to the land beyond the horizon. Without rain, the people would have no crops, and without crops, they would have no food to eat. I can't change the clouds because a Sunbeam is afraid of them."

"But what will I do?" pleaded the little Wave. "She's counting on me to save her."

"Save her from what?" bellowed the Wind impatiently.

"From the darkness," replied the little Wave. "She is afraid her light will go out forever and she will disappear if the darkness comes over the water."

"Nonsense!" whirled the Wind. "Silly Sunbeam! Doesn't she know where her light comes from?"

"No sir, I don't think so."

"Ah, my little friend," the Wind whispered gently, "does she not remember who she is? Perhaps she has forgotten. Go and tell her that she has nothing to be afraid of, for although it will seem as though she has disappeared, once the storm clouds have passed, she will shine again."

And with a kindly whoosh, the Wind moved on, guiding the storm clouds toward the land that lay beyond the horizon.

And so the little Wave turned back to the frightened Sunbeam.

"Wh-what did the Wind say?" she stammered.

But before the little Wave could answer, the darkest of the dark clouds covered the last opening in the sky and the Sunbeam was gone, in an instant, without leaving a trace, and without even a chance to say good-bye.

With the sudden loss of his best friend, the little Wave became afraid. He turned and waved furiously at the elements around him.

"I hate you!" he screamed to the dark sky hovering above.

"I hate you!" he bellowed to the Ocean, now one mass of churning waves.

"I hate you!" he shrieked after the howling Wind.

In his heart, he was terrified. He was afraid he would be swallowed by the great Ocean. He was afraid he would disappear without a trace, like the Sunbeam. But, determined not to give up, he said to himself: "I'll fight until the last. They won't get me!"

All through the night he battled against the mighty Ocean. Each time he was pushed *this* way, he tried to go *that* way. Every time a mighty swell lifted him into the air, he pushed and fought against it as hard as he could. But since he himself was a part of that very same swell, where was there to go? Fearful and angry, he fought, not knowing that he was fighting against himself, for how can a wave be separate from the Ocean?

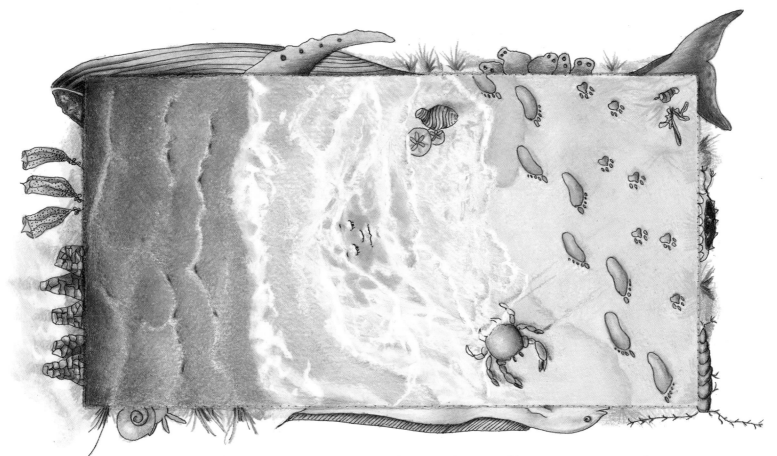

At last, exhausted, he gave up. "I have done all I can. Do with me what you will. I don't care anymore."

In the distance he heard an awful roar. Suddenly a great swell lifted him high, and he could see that he was being carried toward a line of huge rocks. "Oh, no!" he cried. "I'm going to crash into those rocks. This is the end."

The little Wave was lifted high into the air once more and did indeed crash into the rocks.

But it wasn't the end.

He wasn't a little wave anymore, though; he became drops of water and ran down the sides of a rock. "Hello, Rock, you feel so smooth!" he said. "You must be very strong. Are you ticklish?" And he felt the rock wiggle just a little.

He became white foam and played on the beach. "What an interesting place! The sand feels so soft to touch! And there are so many pretty shells!"

21

He became a fine misty spray and danced with the Wind. "Oh, Wind, so this is how it feels to be free and whirl and twirl in the air. Whee!" He laughed with a thousand happy voices.

And for the time being, he forgot about being a little wave, and being the biggest or the most important didn't matter anymore at all. For the first time ever, he wasn't afraid. He felt free, and that was more wonderful than he had ever imagined.

And then he felt something else, something very different. He felt the currents of the Ocean calling him back. "Come home," they beckoned. "This is what you are. Come home."

He stretched himself out and felt the support of millions of droplets of water—the same ones that formed his crest and shaped his curve day after day, and he knew that he had never been alone. He realized that he was part of the great, unending Ocean and that no matter how scary things might seem at times, nothing could hurt him. He was always where he belonged. Even if he changed into foam or misty spray, he would still be himself.

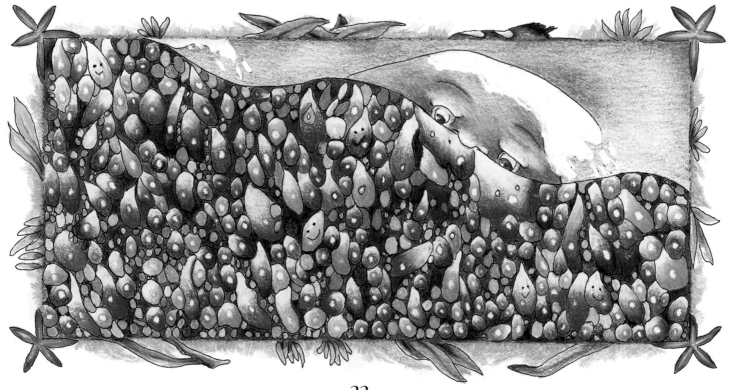

With a sigh of relief, he relaxed and allowed himself to be rocked into a deep and peaceful sleep.

The next day, as soon as the Great Light appeared on the horizon, the tiny Sunbeam slid across the sky with a loud "Whee!" and bounced down right on the crest of the little Wave, knocking him out of a deep sleep.

"Wake up, wake up, wake up!" she laughed, tugging on his white cap. "We have something very important to talk about!" She began to do somersaults down his back.

"Huh?" said the little Wave, still half asleep. Somersaults? The Sunbeam he knew never, ever did somersaults! The little Wave's eyes popped open. Seeing his old friend safe again, he shouted: "You're here! You're back!"

"Of course I'm here!" laughed the Sunbeam.

"I thought you had gone forever and that I would never see you again," said the little Wave.

"So did I," the Sunbeam admitted with a grin. "I looked up at the Great Light in the Daytime Sky and I thought an awful monster was going to get me, but instead, a ray of light reached down to me, and a voice said: "Don't be afraid. You are a part of the Great Light.""

"I didn't know you thought the Great *Light* was a monster," said the little Wave. "I thought the *Ocean* was a monster that was going to swallow *me* up."

"You, too?" she said. "Why didn't you ever tell me?"

"I didn't want you to know I wasn't as mighty as the Ocean," said the little Wave.

"And I didn't want you to know I wasn't the brightest light in all the sky," said the Sunbeam shyly.

"Still want to be friends?" he ventured timidly.

"Yes," nodded the Sunbeam. "Best friends forever!"

And the Sunbeam turned and looked up at the sky and smiled. "I'm a part of the Great Light, and I am loved."

The little Wave looked at the vast Ocean around him and smiled. "Me, too," he said.

And in the days that followed, the little Wave and the tiny
Sunbeam rode the Ocean currents together, carefree and happy, for
the Sunbeam knew herself as a part of the Great Light and the Wave
knew himself as a part of the Ocean.

Both understood that they were home and safe and loved wherever the currents took them, for they were a part of the Majesty of Everything and everything was a part of them.

27

PS:

The next time you look out over the Ocean, notice how the Wind plays tag with the waves and how the sunbeams dance for the Sun. And on a quiet moonlit night you may hear the giggles of a thousand moonbeams reminding you that wherever you are, you are home and safe and loved and part of the Majesty of Everything.

About the Author

Harriet Hamilton grew up in Europe and later lived in Mexico. She is a former writer/producer/director for a Peabody award-winning children's radio station in Little Rock, Arkansas. She resides in Fayetteville, Arkansas, and is the mother of three. She follows the spiritual teachings of Sri Svami Purna, Unity, and *A Course in Miracles*, and has been a member of Unity for ten years.

Harriet says *The Sunbeam and the Wave* is "an example of how the Universe makes a pearl out of an irritation." Visiting a friend in Florida, Harriet was upset one evening about having too many dishes to wash after the friend had cooked. "The very least you could do is to read me something while I clean up *your* mess," she recalls hissing. Her friend opened *A Course in Miracles* to the section entitled "The Little Garden" and began to read. "All of a sudden the characters came alive in my imagination and the mess in the kitchen disappeared. Three days later when I returned home, the story wrote itself."

To reach Harriet by e-mail: hhamil1050@aol.com.

About the Illustrator

Connie Bowen has always loved to draw and majored in art at Washington State University. She works in colored pencil combined with pen and ink. She began creating children's books in 1995 with *I Believe in Me*, which was inspired by her son Matthew and which won the national Athena Award for Excellence in Mentoring. This was followed in 1998 by *I Turn to the Light*. She and her husband Mike and son live in Portland, Oregon.

To check Connie on-line: www.europa.com/~cbowen.

About Wee Wisdom® Books

Unity House's growing line of Wee Wisdom Books is named after the popular children's magazine begun by Unity cofounder Myrtle Fillmore in 1893 and published until 1991.

In founding and editing the magazine, Myrtle was responding to an inner voice that asked her, "Who will take care of the children?"

The Wee Wisdom books—to use Myrtle's own words to describe the magazine stories—are for children "who will be ready to hear and profit by the teachings of Truth in simple story and lesson form that will bring health, happiness, and prosperity" into their entire lives.

As the motto for Wee Wisdom affirms, the books also are for "the child within us all."

The Wee Wisdom series of picture books began in 1992 with *Ted Bear's Magic Swing*, written by Dianne Baker and illustrated by Ronda Krum.

The series also includes *I Believe in Me* and *I Turn to the Light*, books of healing affirmations written and illustrated by Connie Bowen, and *Adventures of the Little Green Dragon*, a deluxe edition of ten stories originally published in *Wee Wisdom* magazine, written by Mari Privette Ulmer and illustrated by Mary Kurnick Maass.

116-0930-10M-3-00